D0687189

076348

A   Aliki
      Overnight at Mary Bloom's.

Colusa County Free Library

738 Market Street
Colusa, CA   95932
Phone: 458-7671

CUP

RLIN

Overnight at Mary Bloom's

Hello?

by ALIKI

Greenwillow Books, New York

*The full color art was created with black
pen-and-ink line combined with watercolor
paints, crayons, and colored pencils.
The text type is Weiderman Book.*

*Copyright © 1987 by Aliki Brandenberg
All rights reserved. No part of this book
may be reproduced or utilized in any form
or by any means, electronic or mechanical,
including photocopying, recording or by
any information storage and retrieval
system, without permission in writing
from the Publisher, Greenwillow Books,
a division of William Morrow & Company, Inc.,
105 Madison Avenue, New York, N.Y. 10016.
Printed in Hong Kong by South China Printing Co.*

First Edition   *10 9 8 7 6 5 4 3 2 1*

Library of Congress Cataloging-in-Publication Data

*Aliki.   Overnight at Mary Bloom's
Summary: A child has a wonderful time when she spends
the night at her grown-up friend's apartment.
[1. Friendship—Fiction.   2. Night—Fiction]   I. Title.
PZ7.A397Ov 1987   [E]   86-7719
ISBN 0-688-06764-6
ISBN 0-688-06765-4 (lib. bdg.)*

For the one and only
Mary Bloom

"Come spend the night," said Mary Bloom.
"We'll have some fun."

So I packed my bag as quickly as I could.

"Just in time," said Mary Bloom.

We cooked

and tossed

and had a feast

fit for a queen.

We washed

and dried

and fed the pets.

"That was just the beginning,"
said Mary Bloom.

We played Dress Up

and Puppet Show.

We played Hide and Seek

and Make a Loud Rumpus.

"It's getting late," said Mary Bloom.

We played Walk the Dogs.

We played Change the Clothes,

Brush the Teeth,

Read the Book,

and Good Night Light.

We snuggled in

and slept like lambs

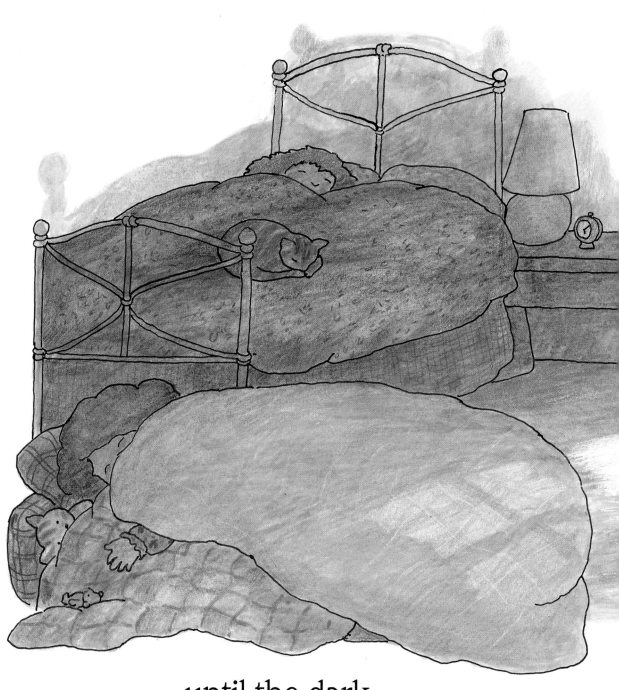

until the dark

became light

and Lucas cried,

"Good morning, Mary."